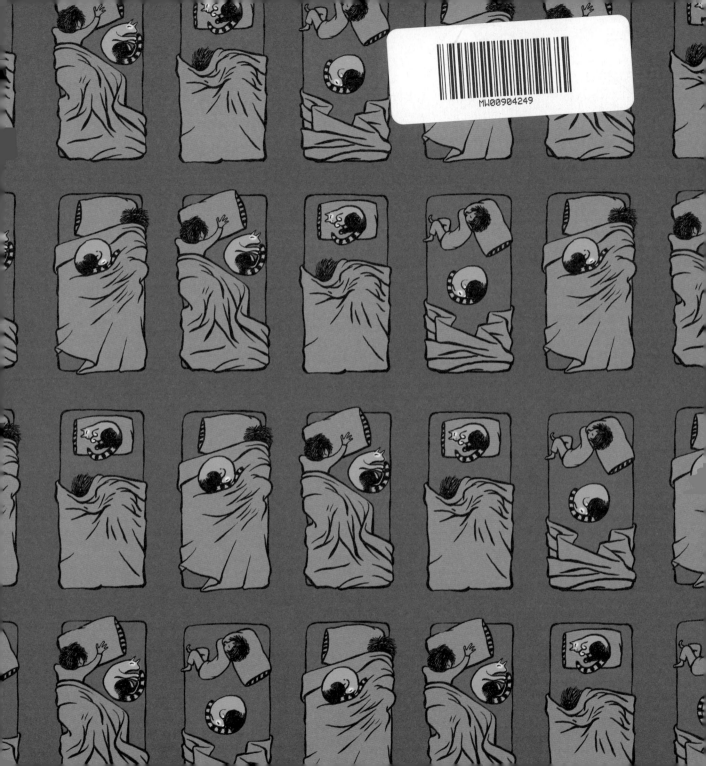

Musta Notta Gotta Lotta sleep last night

For Pierce and Perri
– W.H.P.

For Rip Van Winkle
– G.H.

Musta Notta Gotta Lotta Sleep Last Night
Copyright ©2010 Wendy Hundere Parnell and Guy Hundere

Musta Notta Gotta Lotta is used with the permission of Joe Ely.

Published by Rocket Star Press, Dripping Springs, Texas   www.rocketstarpress.com

Publisher's Cataloging-In-Publication Data
(Prepared by The Donohue Group, Inc.)

Parnell, Wendy Hundere.   Musta notta gotta lotta sleep last night /
[Wendy Hundere Parnell ; illustrated by Guy Hundere] -- 1st ed.

p. : col. ill. ; cm.
Summary: Buddy Brown is very tired at school because his cat kept him from getting
a good night's sleep and now he is having a crazy day that is full of surprises.
Interest age level: 004-008.
ISBN: 978-0-9845843-0-7

1. Cats--Juvenile fiction. 2. Sleep--Juvenile fiction. 3. Cats--Fiction. I. Hundere, Guy. II. Title.

PZ7.P3764 Mu 2010

[E]   2010929941

Part of the Tree Neutral® program, which offsets the number of trees consumed in
the production and printing of this book by taking proactive steps, such as planting
trees in direct proportion to the number of trees used: www.treeneutral.com.

Printed in China on acid-free paper

10 11 12 13 14 15   10 9 8 7 6 5 4 3 2

First Edition

TreeNeutral®

Musta Notta Gotta Lotta sleep last night

written by
Wendy Hundere Parnell

illustrated by
Guy Hundere

inspired by the music of
Joe Ely

ROCKETSTAR
P R E S S

With his cat, Lucky, sleeping soundly on his head
little Buddy Brown tossed in bed.

Fitfully he slept, dreaming of a big toy store,
when startled by the alarm clock he crashed to the floor.

Yawning and sighing and rubbing his head
he grunted and mumbled to himself and said,

"Musta notta gotta lotta sleep last night."

He shook his head and tried to think straight,
remembered it was Friday and school starts at eight.
With his shirt on backwards and his shoes on the wrong feet
he trudged downstairs to the table to eat.

Buddy poured the cereal until it spilled to the floor.
Forming a great heap, he continued to pour.

Unaware of his mistake
and the mess he had made,
he ate his cereal with a fork
in a sleep-deprived haze.

Next he picked up what he thought was his backpack strap
but what Buddy had grabbed was the tail of his cat.

Strangely enough, Lucky didn't protest or fuss
when Buddy slung him over his shoulder and boarded
the school bus.

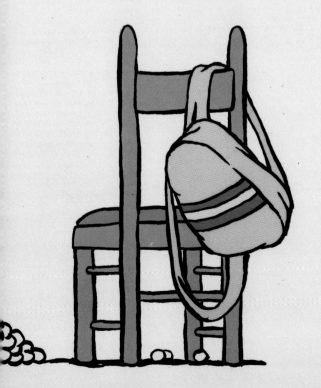

As he got off the bus Buddy wondered, "Where's my stuff?"
He had a strange feeling that this day would be rough.

He still did not notice his cat following behind,
for an adventurous day Lucky was hoping to find.

Sure enough, at school things got worse instead of better
when the teacher called on Buddy who was asleep
and couldn't tell her which letter
came after C and A to spell the word CAT.

His teacher wanted to know
just what Buddy made of that.

Confused and groggy
Buddy lifted his head,
then sheepishly muttered softly
and said,

**"Musta notta gotta lotta
sleep last night."**

hat sat
flat s mat cat

The teacher gave Buddy a disapproving look.
While rapping her fingernails on his book
she said,
    "Must not have gotten
    a lot of sleep last night?
That I should say sounds about right!"

    Buddy braced himself
    for what he feared was to come,
    a trip to the principal's office
    or maybe a call to his mom.

But before the teacher could say anything more...

...a big fat pig came charging through the door!

It seems Cool Rockin' Loretta's pet pig had followed her too.
The classroom was beginning to look and behave like a zoo
as Buddy's curious cat that had been lurking nearby
saw the large hoofed animal and wanted a ride.

The cat jumped onto the pig and held on tight

like a bronco bull rider
having the ride of his life.

Flipping,
flopping,
and bouncing
to no end,

Lucky moved like a leaf twisting in the wind.

"That's Roadhawg!" shouted Loretta after her swine.
"Somebody help me, please. Stop that pig of mine!"

As class erupted in uproarious laughter
no one could guess just what would come after.

The class began to chase after the pig with the cat.
They raced around desks snaking this way and that.

They followed like boxcars behind an out of control train,
everyone acting absurd and somewhat insane.

Except the teacher,
who stood frozen
with her mouth wide open
thinking, "I don't understand.
How did this all happen?"

And Buddy so tired he thought it might all be a dream
and maybe things couldn't really be as they seem.

Blinking his eyes and shaking his head
Buddy pinched himself in disbelief as he said,

"Musta notta gotta lotta sleep last night."

Then the boy with the bright yellow hair,
who calls himself Crazy Lemon, stood on his chair
and crowed like a rooster at the top of his lungs.

Everyone *stopped* to see what on earth was going on.

Even Roadhawg, the pig,
and Lucky, the cat
stopped in surprise
at the odd sound of that.

Then the two animals ran out the door and away.
The school bell rang. That was it for the day.

On the bus home next to Buddy sat Billy the Kid,
the boy who lived down the street and liked to talk big.

"I taught my chihuahua to sing," boasted Billy the Kid.
Buddy thought, "Oh, yeah, well *my* cat can ride a pig."

To be nice Buddy asked, "What song?"
When he got no answer, Buddy whispered,
"No wonder we never got along."

"What did you say?" gruffed Billy the Kid.
"Did you say something? I know you did."

Diverting his eyes and lowering his head,
Buddy gave a weak smile and smugly said,

"Musta notta gotta lotta sleep last night."

Dinner and a bath, it was finally time for bed.
Buddy put on his pajamas and laid down his head.

He had his hopes up high for a good night of sleep.
Another day like today he did not want to repeat.

But the next morning went just like the one before.

Again he poured his cereal all over the floor.

Buddy's mom looked at the mess in dismay
then tenderly asked her son, "Buddy, are you okay?"

Rubbing his eyes and nodding his head,
Buddy put his arms around
his mommy and said,

"Please understand me.
Everything's all right.
I just **musta notta
gotta lotta sleep
last night**."

Today would be different though for Buddy Brown,
who ate his breakfast...

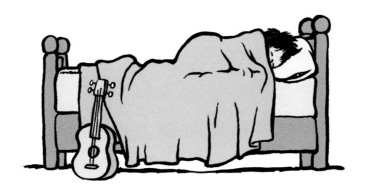

and laid back down.

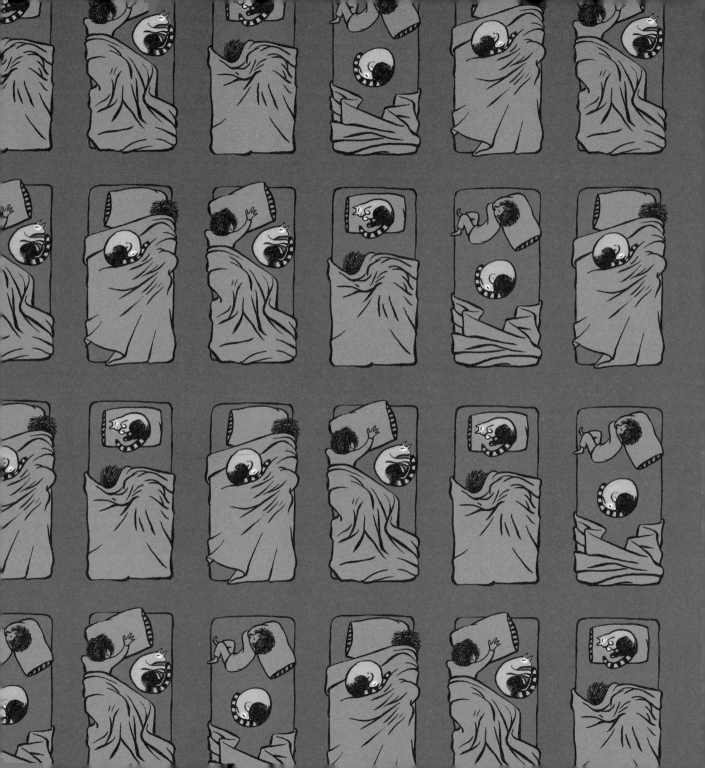